Alligator Resort

Copyright © Nick Voro 2024

All rights reserved. No part of this publication may be reproduced or transmitted in any form or by any means, electronic or mechanical, including photocopying, recording, or any information storage and retrieval system, without permission in writing from the publisher.

First Edition

Alligator Resort

VoroBooks, Etobicoke, Ontario, Canada

ISBN: 978-1-7383199-4-7

Typesetting and additional design by Lee Thompson Editing+

To contact the author: Nick_Voro@hotmail.com

This is a work of fiction. Names, characters, places and incidents either are products of the author's imagination or are used fictitiously. Any resemblance to actual events or locales or persons, living or dead, is entirely coincidental.

ALLIGATOR RESORT

I AM A SARCASTIC ASSHOLE with a mocking sense of humor. I am also a user of people. Usually those closest to me. I collect their personal information. I drain them. Among all the well-known things a friend or a lover does, I go a step further, and do what one should never do— take what I am told in utter confidence and use it against the very people who have told it to me.

Yes, I am perfectly sane, fully aware of my

actions. Nothing is ever done in a moment of estrangement from self, or capricious lapsing into passion. I know what I am doing and why I am doing it, I understand the consequences, and yet I carry on.

This is real life after all, and there will always be casualties. So whether strangers, vaguely familiar acquaintances I met at some cocktail party, childhood friends with whom I played croquet on their father's newly-acquired estate's lawn, or spent semesters roomed up with in the same Harvard dorm, all that ceases to matter as they become my informants (non-consensual and without a formal agreement, of course), adding that touch of authenticity to my grandiose projects.

The realization of treachery and betrayal only sinks in after they read my latest bestseller (name change being only a preventative measure until they inevitably catch on) and see their private lives publicly broadcast, accessible to anyone willing to spend a few bucks to fulfill a voyeuristic characteristic everyone has (no matter how seemingly different we are from one another). I copyright their lives as a figment of my boundless artistic imagination, which I use—albeit at a very leisurely pace—to produce original albeit slightly fabricated imitations of life.

If my publishers only knew... Well, even then I doubt they would care, as long as this information didn't leak to the press (I seal my lips). Because if it did, that is a stock-market-crash slide in sales and a bunch of lawsuits I hardly want to deal with. I am imagining they probably do not either. My lawyer fees alone would be an extravagant figure with plenty of zeros, conceivably the sum total of my last three publishing-house paychecks. I might be rich, but no one is rich enough for a lawyer's blood.

So, I finish this confession to my psychiatrist (talking to clinicians in confined spaces solves a good deal of what is left unsaid in the wide-open spaces of real life... usually), stating that the dust jackets of my novels denounce any real-life connections. And you know what he says? Nothing.

Absolutely nothing. Yellow pad in hand, he simply continues to scribble a Picasso-worthy sketch with a watercolor pencil.

I am neither a fortune-teller nor am I as intuitive as a woman, but looking at the latest vessel spread in the *Yachting Magazine* lying open on his mahogany desk, I can only assume it's a sketch of his next boat. Or the one he already owns, and now he is compulsively comparing, sketch-filling in its shortcomings, which he has realized while window shopping other lusciously illustrated yachts just slightly out of his price range.

He has no answers for me. No solutions for any of my problems. On a good note, he has a suggestion. He recommends heartily that I take a vacation, which he himself is going to do soon—probably sail around the world on his yacht.

But who am I to judge; I should be frank and say these mind-stabilizing sessions are paid for by my parents. They sponsor most of my lifestyle, including paying for my aristocratic downtown loft, thinking my job to be more of a hobby than someone's actual life's work. My personal cash-caretakers with hearts of financial gold. Their digit, no-strings-attached love knows few boundaries and their monthly allowances keep me afloat even though I can keep myself afloat. The best part: my amassed literary fortune keeps growing, bypassing the usual lifestyle reductions thanks to the willing nature of these parental units. A win-win for everyone.

I take a minute to ponder this near-mute medical practitioner's getaway suggestion and come up with the perfect spot—the family cottages. As they say, "If you can't face your problems, run away."

A few days later, I am in the back seat of my parents' first bought car, before their ascent to status—a Volkswagen Beetle—a crammed criminally compact car created at the behest of the German Führer (with his expansion and enslavement plans for much of Europe, I am baffled he did not design a roomier auto). So much for running...

Most would attribute my father's choice to hold on to the mint 1970s vehicle as a sign of nostalgia, a humbling reminder of one's roots no matter how high you climb. The reality is much simpler. My father has never thrown out a single thing in his life, living his all-American hoarding dream. And so we were off in the hoarder's vehicle of choice toward a perfectly idyllic location for some well-deserved recreational rest.

I know it sounds rather ridiculous, but I am not even dressed properly—Armani sports jacket and Gucci loafers. What a nightmare. My multi-millionaire banker father gripping the steering wheel and next to him Mother, who has her own cooking show, with some underhanded feminist views. A plagiaristic Bestselling Author, a Shady Banker, and a Television Personality slash Leading Activist for women's lib—the *Three's Company* gang from cable reruns with one sex reassignment surgery for the analogy to work and minus the edgy late-70s double entendres riding around in the Führer's sardine can of a car.

An indefinite period later (that feels like an eternity), we arrive and blessedly I no longer have to listen to Mother hum Janis Joplin songs and Father make frequent urgent phone calls to his business partner (who is probably his mistress).

As I step out of the car, fresh air rushes upward my nose. Air virginal and undefiled by large fossil fuel companies and their steady climate-changing contributions. This freshness is new to me. I am a city dweller after all, used to ensconcing in darkness, breathing pollutants and ingesting Schedule II drugs.

My most reoccurring imagery is of neon-lit warehouses where the next your-presence-is-required party is happening. Where glow sticks make up for a vital assembly-stic part of some probably underage girl's latest Nicole Miller two-piece.

I feel claustrophobic among the ancient giants, the natural force of Mother Nature overwhelming me, agitating the remnants of illegally obtained substances still coursing through my bloodstream. I feel a gravitational pull. Invisible forces seize hold of my soul and tear it from my body, leaving behind just the shell, cadaverous and incomplete.

No matter where I have gone my whole life, I have always felt a violent pressure to fit in, project-ing something I am not through a made-up per-sonality. Here I am compelled to confront a part of me I left behind—my innocent adolescence.

What strange revelations fresh air can have on a person. Here in the heartland of America, in its woods, I suddenly feel nostalgia for my child-hood. Surely there is a secret foundry, hidden deep in the forest, releasing scents of sentimentality, evoking the alluring recollection of some Camp Scout's burnt marshmallows...

The following afternoon I awake in my old room, confronted by dusty bookshelves and monstrous stuffed animals. I lie in bed recollecting the past evening with my father, his prolonged attempt to ignite a campfire. Okay, so he did not strike two rocks belonging to the flint family—Aristocrats and Neanderthals are vastly different groups after all, belonging to different social classes. He still did better than I ever thought possible, and I applauded his efforts all the same for even mustering enough interest to attempt this. I shift my thoughts back to myself (how typical). My body aches from a contorted sleeping position, my vision is blurry and my fingers are cramping with what must be early signs of arthritis. On top of this laundry list of complaints, I have a full bladder from all the imported beer last night. Not a good start to the day.

So while in the bathroom taking care of that unsavory business a man of letters should never be overly explicit about in his writing unless toilet humor makes a grand comeback, I happen to look out the window to witness a congregation—don't ask me for quantitative data, I didn't count them—of alligators slithering on the meticulously manicured lawn below and dirtying the adjacent ultramarine lake (and its esteemed crystal-clear

clarity) with their predominating greenery, caus-
ing me to stare in sheer disbelief from this mod-
ernistic chic cabin erected by a renowned architect who had a penchant for taking your ideas,
completely disregarding them and delivering a
building tailored to his own vision—a building
that is aesthetically pleasing but completely use-
less as a stronghold.

I steadily back away from the window, back
to the present moment, utterly horrified by my
current predicament.

The corner of my right eye catches sight of
the living room's doorframe, the safety of another
room making me relax prematurely. Then the same
eye catches another sight, the sight of a Cloaked
Figure lurking down the hallway.

If anyone ever wanted an accurate depiction
of the Grim Reaper, this guy was the personifica-
tion of Death. Bloodshot bulging eyes, jet black hair
matted with sweat, and body draped in black with
extremely pale hands and grossly protruding veins.

Around his waist is a leather belt with a

holster housing a positively menacing handgun, possibly a Beretta, known for its deadly accuracy and relentless reliability (but this is just a guess from a non-gun enthusiast and First Amendment gospeler).

I want to call him fraudulent, a product of a make-believe world, an embodiment of my worst fears, but his presence quickly cripples me with an overspreading sensation of dread.

My head begins to throb, the once-safe living room becomes noticeably hotter, even scorching, and I feel a blinding notion enter my mind: purification from sin is through punishment, and he is here to punish me (and therefore save me).

Eventually, I reject the momentary proselytism spurred by this escapee from the nether regions, come to and sprint for the bathroom, bolting the door, entrusting my life to a flimsy lock (avant-garde architects never do seem to care for security).

Outstanding; simply outstanding! Singled out and confined to my bathroom, incredulous as I overlook a gator wasteland, a reptile-strewn lawn leading to a single road that is the only direct passageway to my parents' cabin, unless of course I feel a surge of heroism and act on my parallel alternative of making it safely across the lake by canoe (my parents sojourn at a much swankier cabin across the lake, one designed by a much superior architect I might add)… but surely once I get a paddle in the water, they will grab me and haul my body with their powerfully sharp jaws into the murky depths of the lake, suffocation by immersion, expelling what remaining oxygen I have and submerging, submerging….

A knock interrupts my fleeting sinking feeling and horrible visions of frantic paddling, alligators ramming, a capsized canoe and gut-wrenching human screams for help in gator-infested waters. My passing thought: at least he has enough manners to knock. And since I fail to ask him in, as should come as no great surprise, the pounding only intensifies, with his fist now connecting with the door. He never even bothers with the handle.

Either he knows better, or... he knows me. In the grand scheme of things, believability already stretching to the snapping point, could he not be one of those I depleted, stole from, drained? One of those I have used and flung away? Someone whose trust I betrayed, breaking the inviolable rule of every strong and true friendship? And has this violation, betrayal, alienation, perhaps induced such profound hurt to cause the donning of a *cloche*? Have I pushed a man to conceive a devious plan with devilish determination to end the orderly life of a best-selling life-plagiarizing novelist? The door shudders, its laborious life of constantly opening and closing coming to an end. I brace myself. Any moment now it will con-cede defeat to this bestial besieging. His foot is obviously at work here. Delivering impassioned declarative kicks. The door moves inward, putting pressure on the hinges. Yes, yes, any moment now. My beacon of hope will plunge into darkness. I need divine inspiration. I need something... soon... instantaneously. I am inexperienced with the whole survival-tactic routine, cognizant that this makes me the wrong candidate for the job. But this hindrance greatly affects my inheritance. And I must, at all costs, prolong my existence long enough to cash my parents' life insurance policy. I will not allow disinheritance through premature death.

With the policy as a motivational driver, I step to the window casement. I place one foot firmly on the bathtub, boost myself up and sit down on the ledge of the window. The bathroom door keeps shuddering, about to disintegrate, taking numerous kicks from the Cloaked Figure, who apparently has the legs of a bodybuilder and the feet of a football hooligan.

I open the window and swing my feet over.

The ground below overflows with alligators. Now I am not an expert, but these alligators seem larger than your typical swamp dweller and their hostility spurred on by something other than biology, and if I take a real wild guess, I will say it is achieved by a chemical reaction from some good ole human tampering with Mother Nature.

I start edging along the slopped shingled roof of the third story toward the downspout to the right, remaining aware that if I slip, they will devour me. These loathsome reptilians. They seem to sense me and move about anxiously, replicating my movements perfectly. True to their predatory nature, their movements are almost noiseless, making you momentarily forget they are there until you look down and confirm the nightmare is real.

In the distance, I spot my canoe, a swaying siren, tempting me aboard. But it might as well be a mirage. I shake my head. I have no illusions about using it. They can keep up just fine, before ramming and overtaking. I double down on my efforts, believing in no other alternative path.

Our repetition of movement evolves into a rhythm of sorts—I crawl, they mimic; I speed up; they adjust their pace accordingly, my circling copies, tailing me in a never-ending cycle until I have this thought, lose concentration, mentally slip, lose footing, and physically slide, emitting a vigorous cry for help that creeps upwards from the pit of my stomach and through my windpipe, a musical composition to accompany my descent while the whole time clawing at the shingles until I catch hold of the gutter at the last possible min- ute, scrape one hand in the process and helplessly hang there holding on for dear dear life with the other, increasingly trembling and rapidly perspiring.

I feel blood oozing from the cuts on my free-floating hand, dribbling down and exciting the horde below. My other hand is slipping, my arm muscles tightening up. I cannot hold my weight much longer considering my current phys- ical condition, not to mention years of lackluster parenting lacking any actual parental advice, formative years without direction, without those early nuggets of wisdom regarding my future life-sustaining-needs in case of possible survival situations, all leaving me completely unprepared to deal with situations like my present predica- ment where I am called upon to perform one-arm gutter gymnastics and easily swing my way across to safety.

A sharp *bang* explodes behind me, but before I can react, something pierces my shoulder as it travels past my left ear. Upon closer examination, I pronounce it to be a bullet, surpassing the speed of sound and passing through the shooting gallery placard, a.k.a. my shoulder, before embedding itself in the framework of the house. A bullet meaning to take my life. Oh, great! Now he is shooting at me.

For some reason I expected him to follow me through the bathroom window, but he has to be on the ground below, shooting up while I swing around perfectly posed in his crosshairs, readying for my headshot feature on the cover of *Shingle Shenanigans*.

Click. He does not wait long before he fires the weapon again. The next bullet pierces the previously grazed shoulder and causes me to swing forward from the sheer impact of the projectile.

Third time being the charm, and considering

it is a lonely place at the top, I swing forward with what little remains of my strength, plunge forth like a trapeze artist with hope for the best, and land ungracefully on the deck of the second floor, smacking my head.

My thunderous fall initiates an advancing footrace below—what beasts were still in the nearby water now all touch ground, and those already on land rapidly round the corner of the cottage toward the stairs, toward me. A race for the gnawing of the human meat (that's me). I quickly get to my feet; in my head a nightingale is singing its morbid song, announcing my inevitable death. The weapon discharges again. Time is clearly not on my side. I start to run, sprint forward with a marathon runner's finish-line determination, beat the beasts to the side stairs and only come to a full stop once the ancient forest giants with their crowns of green hide me from projectiles and snapping jaws.

The pain I feel is excruciating, spoiling clear-headed thinking, distorting, jumbling all the thoughts inside my head. All I know is I must keep moving. Stopping is not on the itinerary. I must remain in constant motion. It is integral to my survival.

I am also leaving behind a trail the Cloaked Figure will find easy enough to track. I dismiss praying. A silent and unseen god will not answer my payers. He will not pardon me the grim reality of wandering through these labyrinthine trails waiting for the Cloaked Figure or his hell spawn to materialize.

Blindly walking forward, focusing on some imaginary point—when it is all just trees and more trees—I miss the ones that matter: the trees painted to mark a muddy area ahead. And one lame step later, all that it takes before the ground turns to soft wet earth and my legs start to descend into this suffocating sludge.

I have the sinking vision of my sunken body decomposing in the mud, preserved for eternity down to the finest details, such as my grimace of horrid fright. Until, one day, a forester stumbles across my perfectly preserved body, a rare find, a grotesque curiosity destined for a display case at a national museum.

The noise of approaching footsteps, human and alligatorian, breaks my useful reverie. The abundance of trees nearby is my only hope. As I unbuckle my belt, further visions invade my mind, a cluster of invasive, agonizing thoughts. Some involve dismemberment while other frightening flash-forward scenarios focus on evisceration. With terror in my eyes, and a terrible tremor in my hands, and with my personal best rendition of the cool technique of the Marlboro Man, I aim the lasso—my belt, extending into the buckle—as accurately as possible toward a vertical crack in the nearest tree.

I cannot hold back my surprise when it actually works. The buckle, a metallic clasp custom-fitted for the crevice! I give it a firm tug, securing it in place. Then I yank with my good hand, dragging myself out, decreasing the distance to refuge literally one handful at a time.

Once out, I take painstakingly slow steps down a concealed path, encountering my first bit of good luck by coming across an old barn with loosely-hung wide-open doors revealing a Chevrolet pickup rust-box inside. The only research I have ever done for any of my novels (outside of pumping my friends for personal bits of information) was for a pulp novel where the lead character had to hot-wire a car. I put that knowledge to good use. It takes a bit, the starter turns, smoke spews out the exhaust, but eventually a thunderously rattling noise sounds as the engine reanimates (similar to the spark that gave life to Victor Frankenstein's misunderstood monstrous creation). I have no idea why it is there, but I am thankful it is.

I cling to the steering wheel with my trembling hands and back out, turn and head down an L-shaped road. As I round the corner, I experience a sudden bout of paralysis. Ahead, bent at one knee, is the Cloaked Figure, his arms now gripping a state-of-the-art rifle, which he points at my windshield.

I shift to a lower gear and floor it. The Chevrolet races forward as the windshield begins taking direct, silent hits, fracturing as I impassively pierce through his body, all the while sonically imagining the sickening crunch of his bones breaking as he slides below. The truck momentarily lifts, rocking all over the place, passing over the human roadside bump. I fix my eyes on the vastness ahead, never bothering to look back.

With the sun setting, I turn on the headlights. My parents' cabin is not much farther. I can feel the closeness of my destination when, without warning, a jolt forces the old Chevrolet from the forest road. I try my best to compensate for the sudden directional change, but my reflexive steering still results in a head-on collision with a tree.

This development is not in my favor! In fact, the situation is a touch demoralizing. The driver's-side door, taking the full force of a massive alligator's armor-plated tail (as I have now registered), will not budge.

I find myself imprisoned inside a rusting

coffin with commotion all around, courtesy of the swiftly approaching, ravenous, blood-lusting and continuously charging bastard offspring (now that their father, the perpetrator of all this madness, is dead).

A second hit, this time from a different alligator's tail, crushes the passenger door inward. The window dissolves into shards, imploding, puncturing my skin and creating a passageway for a large grotesque head with a salivating mouth. I am covered in blood, choking on it, wanting to give up. But now is not the time to play the role of a sniveling victim airing out all his complaints.

I leap, land on the backseat, rotate my body and start frantically kicking at the rear window until I feel it give. With vigor for survival, I thrust my body through the broken opening, tumble out of the truck's bed and, alligators at my heels, run until I reach my parents' cabin.

The air inside is otherworldly, as if it carries particles responsible for overstimulating these deranged peninsula inhabitants on this fine summer day.

My search of the cottage yields no one. I look out the window expecting the cabin to be surrounded, but there are no gators anywhere. I am alone guarding the fortress, waiting for the Tartars to show up. I open a few windows, allowing fresh air to circulate. Then I sit down, feeling the full force of my exhaustion and my injuries. The adrenaline is wearing off, pain returning. Is it so preposterous to imagine that the mysterious and sinister mastermind, the Cloaked Figure, would abduct my parents and deliver an army of supercharged alligators to my cottage for the sole purpose of testing an immature, egotistical coward? Or am I over-complicating the matter and he simply did not care, fully expecting me not to have made it out alive from the cottage's bathroom?

Trapped again. I need someone... anyone... to come to rescue me (after my futile attempt at rescuing others). I need someone to answer the unexplainable.

Just then, the phone rings.

It is the mismatched married couple from my

favorite sitcom: My Life. And while, my alive-and-well parents talk about everything they bought while shopping in town, never bothering to ask why exactly I am at their cottage, my thoughts are on their life insurance policy, the structural damage to my cabin and the cloak coming away from the maniac's face the moment I hit him with the junker truck; regrettably never fully exposing his face, but more of that matted jet black hair initially revealed during the bathroom ambush. At one point, it even parted, further revealing scalp scarring.

I know that pitch-black hair with the striking scar underneath... And that is not the only thing I know.

I also know he is here. In the room with me. I sense him standing to the side of me, covered in his own blood. I slowly turn to face him, instantaneously proving myself right, a victor and loser at the same moment.

My eyes wander over to his holster. It is empty. His gun seems to be missing. This somewhat reduces the threat.

Along with his missing gun, his cloak is torn to shreds. Is it from the truck swipe or his children turning on their maker, sensing a shift in power? Spotting weakness in an impenetrable tyrannical ruler?

He allows me to continue my restless roaming across his body while he just stands there, in one spot, a motionless monolith, a dark brooding figure, as blood drips down on to the floor, a soothing sort of dripping, leaving stains which will endure at least a couple of cleanings.

Slowly, and with trembling hands, I decide to remove his cloak. I do just that. The purpose behind my actions unknown even to me. Perhaps it is the glimpse of my killer's face, a confirmation of his identity before he slaughters me without a second thought.

The cloak falls behind his head, drapes his shoulders.

Underneath, a yacht is visibly bracing against high winds and stormy sea. It looks abandoned. Unmanned. It is struggling to stay afloat. A tragic sight. One I cannot look away from. I stand and stare as darkness steadily eclipses everything until nothing remains. Not him nor I.

ABOUT THE AUTHOR

A native of Kyiv, Ukraine, but living in Canada since the age of eleven, Nick Voro discovered literature at an early age, never quite mustering the ability to put an excellent book down. A recent graduate of the Toronto Film School, Nick divides his time between being a full-time parent and a full-time author.

His debut work, *Conversational Therapy: Stories and Plays*, has recently sold over 200 copies and is part of the library system (United States, Canada, New Zealand, Australia and Scotland).

Lee D. Thompson, an editor and writer from Moncton, New Brunswick, Canada, edited this short story. His books include: a novel in [xxx] dreams from Broken Jaw Press, Mouth Human Must Die from Frog Hollow Press and Apastoral: A Mistopia from Corona/Samizdat. His short fiction has been published in many anthologies, including Random House's Victory Meat, New Fiction from Atlantic Canada and Vagrant Press's The Vagrant Revue of New Fiction. He is the winner of the David Adams Richards Prize (2018) and New Brunswick Book Award (2022). He is the publisher of Galleon Books.

www.ingramcontent.com/pod-product-compliance
Lightning Source LLC
Chambersburg PA
CBHW071400200726
48294CB00004B/1229